This book belongs to:

_____

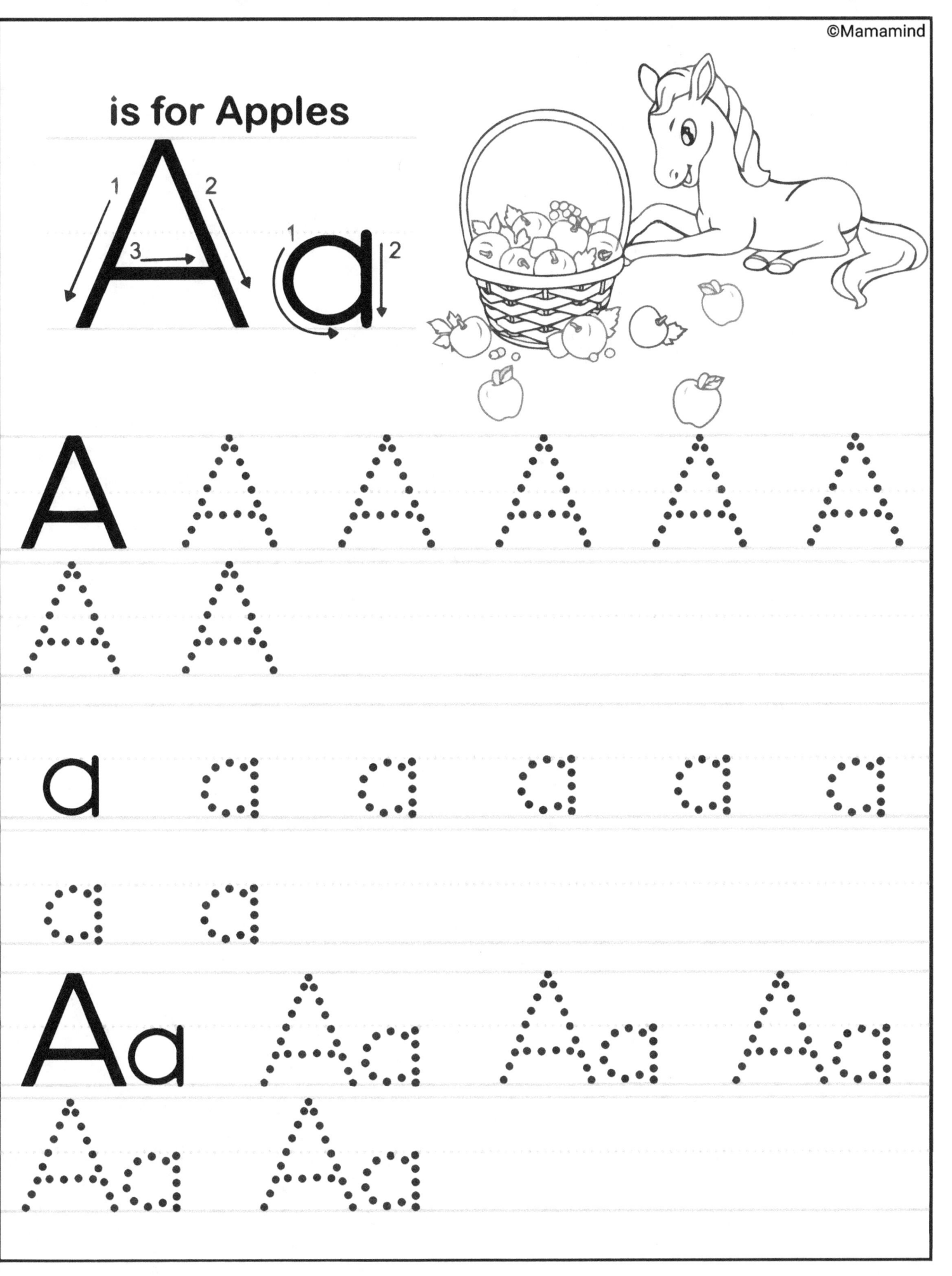

is for Bridle

C is for Canter

is for Dressage

Dd

E is for Eventing

H is for Hay

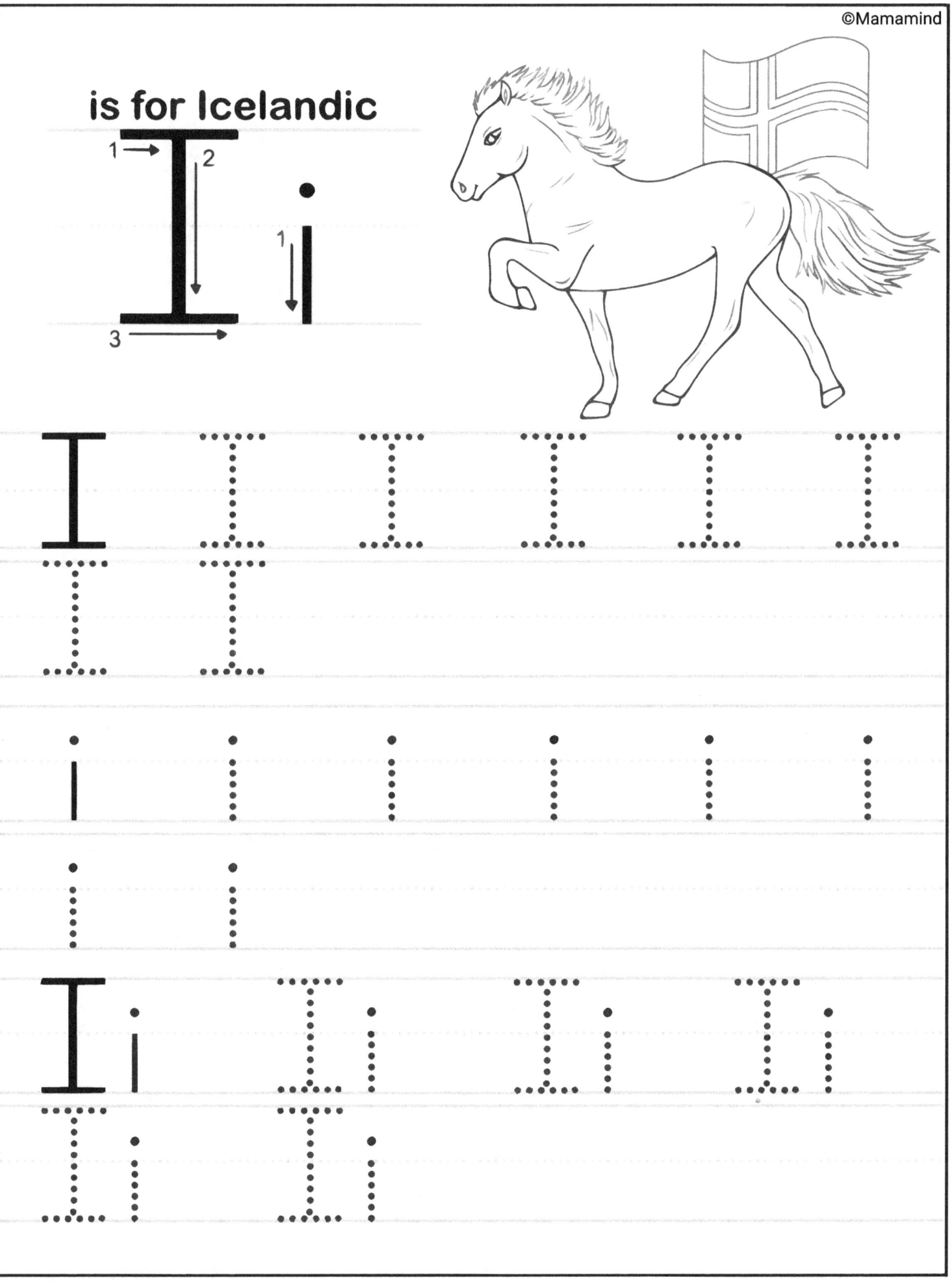

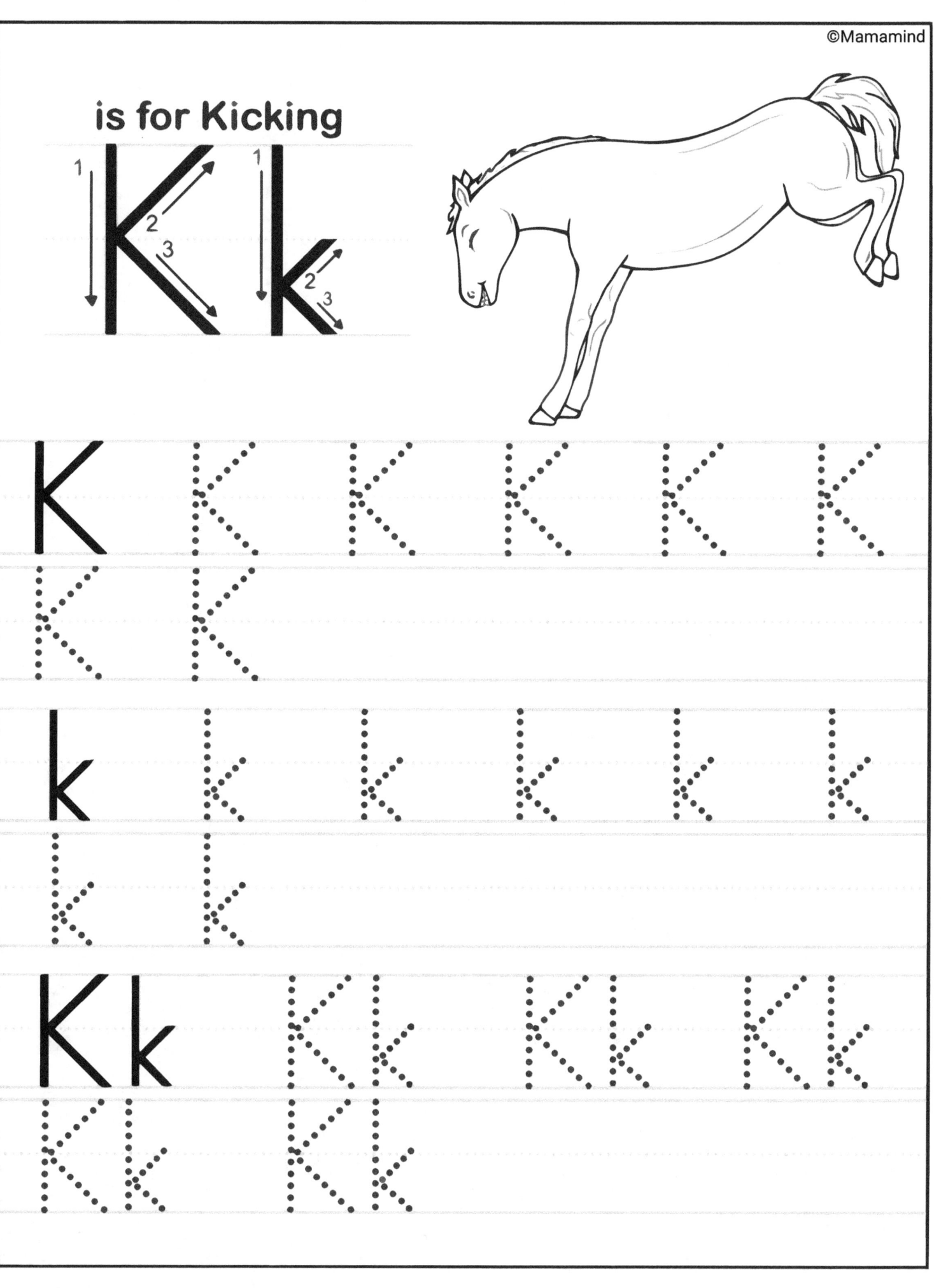

is for Oats

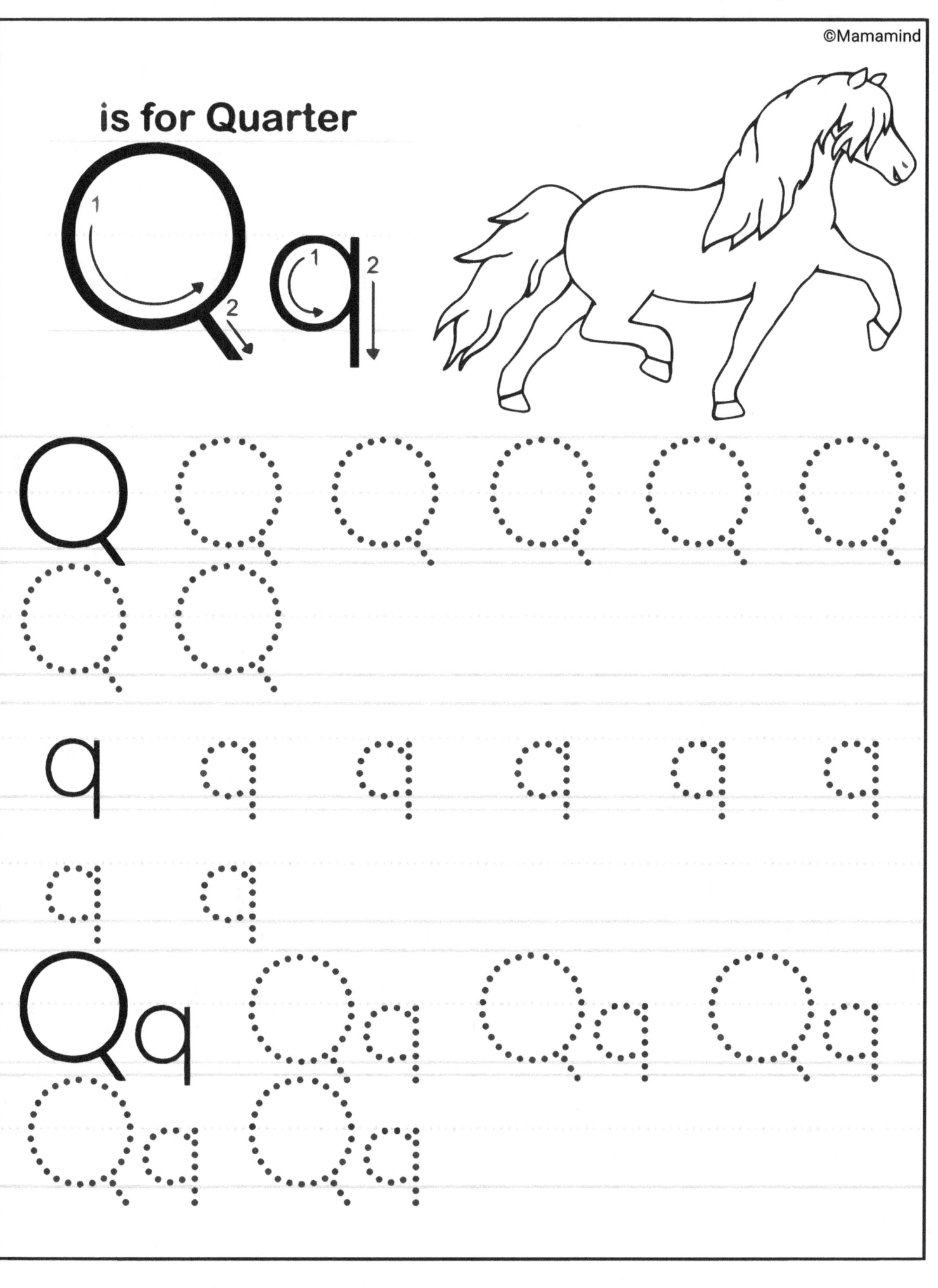

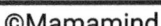

is for Saddle

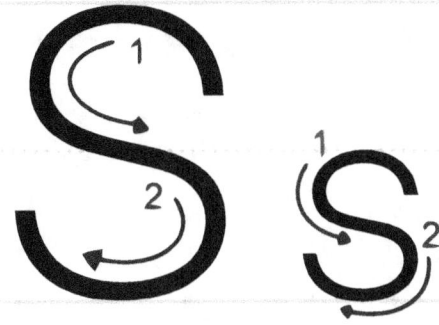

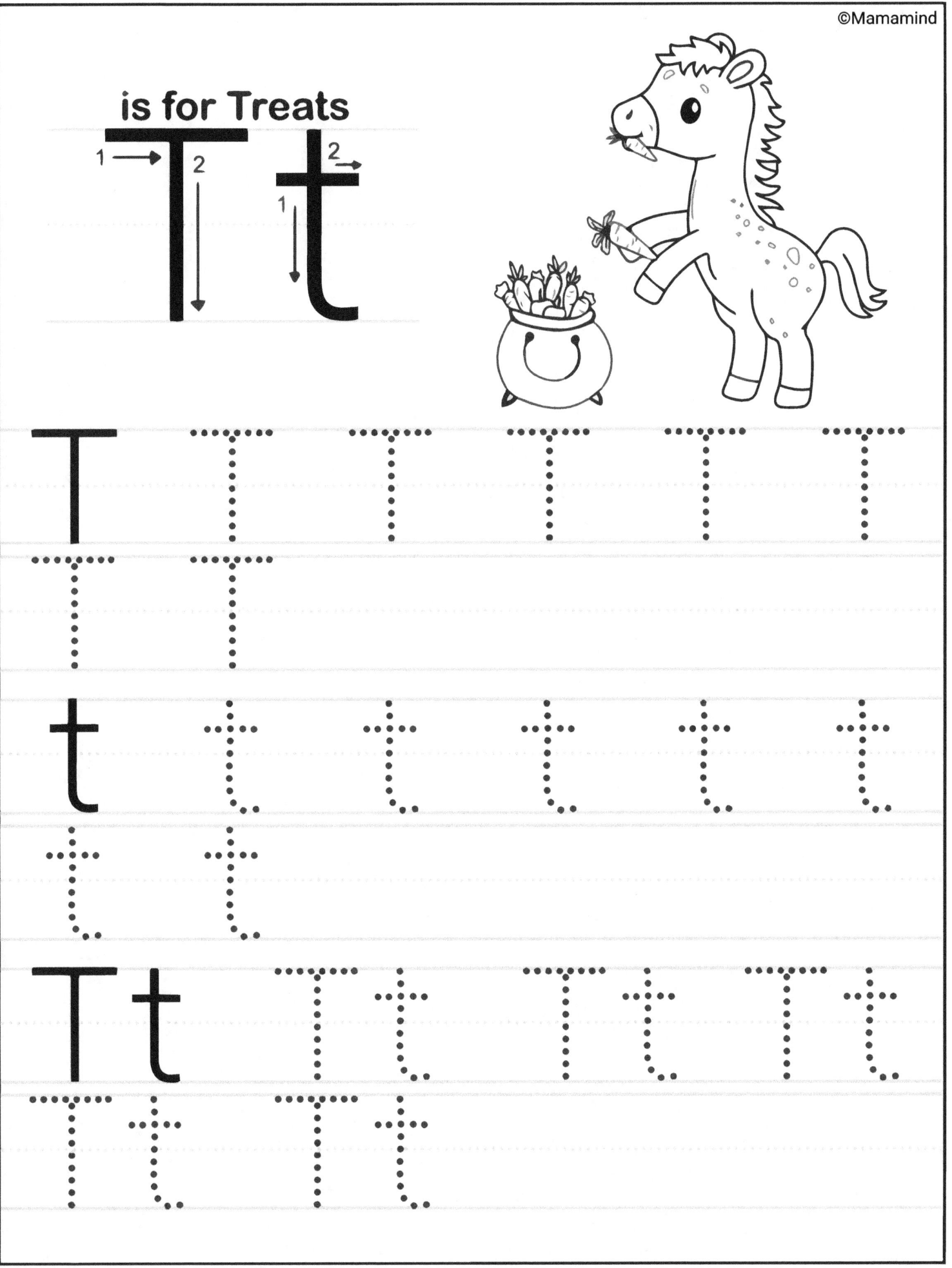

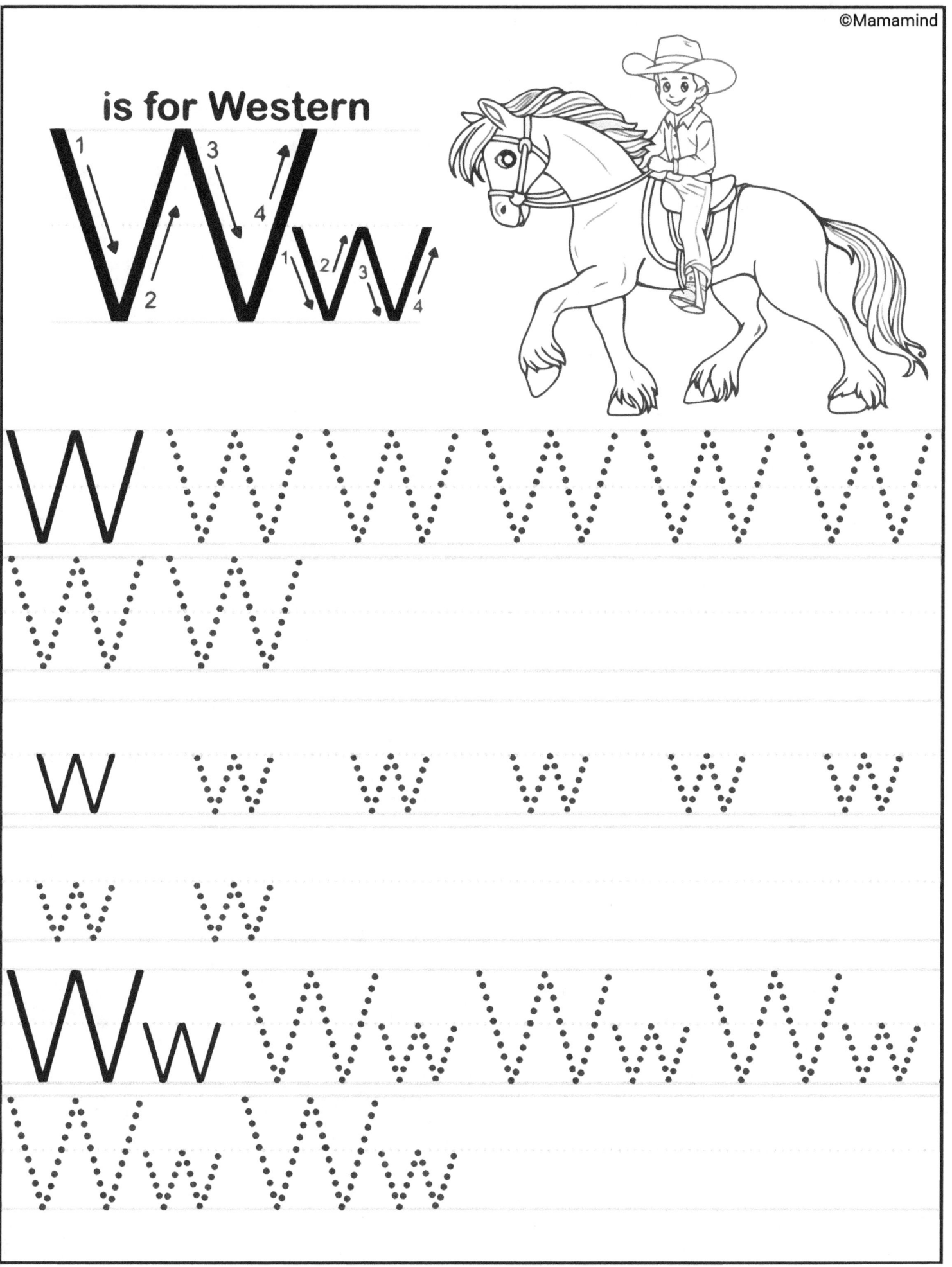

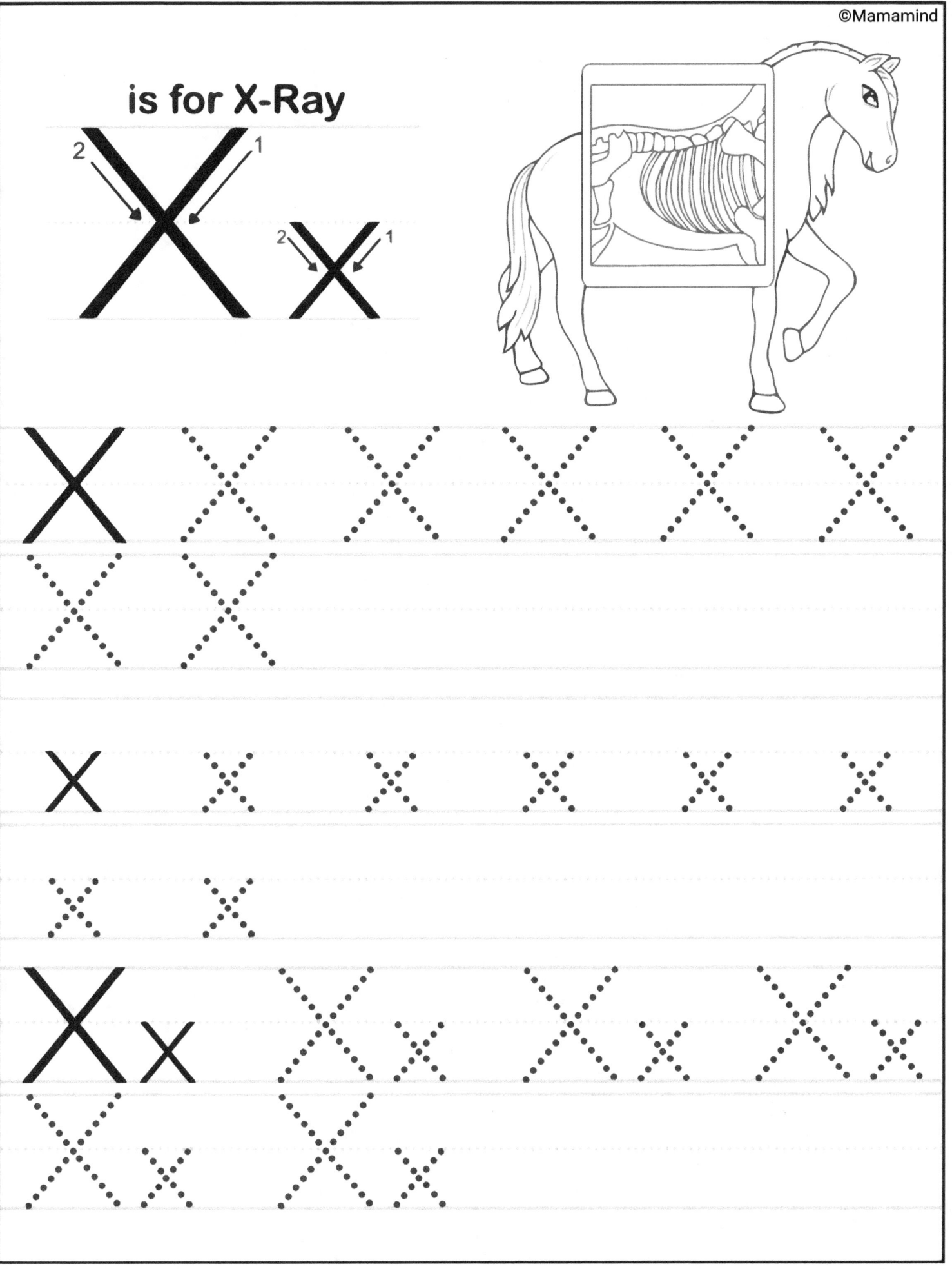

is for Zzzzz

Z z

www.ingramcontent.com/pod-product-compliance
Lightning Source LLC
Chambersburg PA
CBHW082214070526
44585CB00020B/2412